BUILT FOR SPEED

adapted by Bill Scollon

illustrated by Disney Storybook Artists

Reader's Digest
Children's Books

New York, New York • Montréal, Québec • Bath, United Kingdom

Every day, Dusty Crophopper would fly over the crops, spraying them with Vita-minamulch. Dusty was a crop duster, but he dreamed of being a world champion racer!

Dusty practiced every chance he got. "Let's run some obstacles!" shouted his friend, Chug.

Dusty skimmed the treetops. "Woo-hoo!" he cried.

Dusty planned to try out for the Wings Around The Globe Rally. He asked Skipper, a war hero who'd flown hundreds of missions, if he would be his coach. "Go home, kid," said the cranky old plane. "You're in over your head."

At the tryouts, Dusty got his first look at the three-time world champion, Ripslinger!

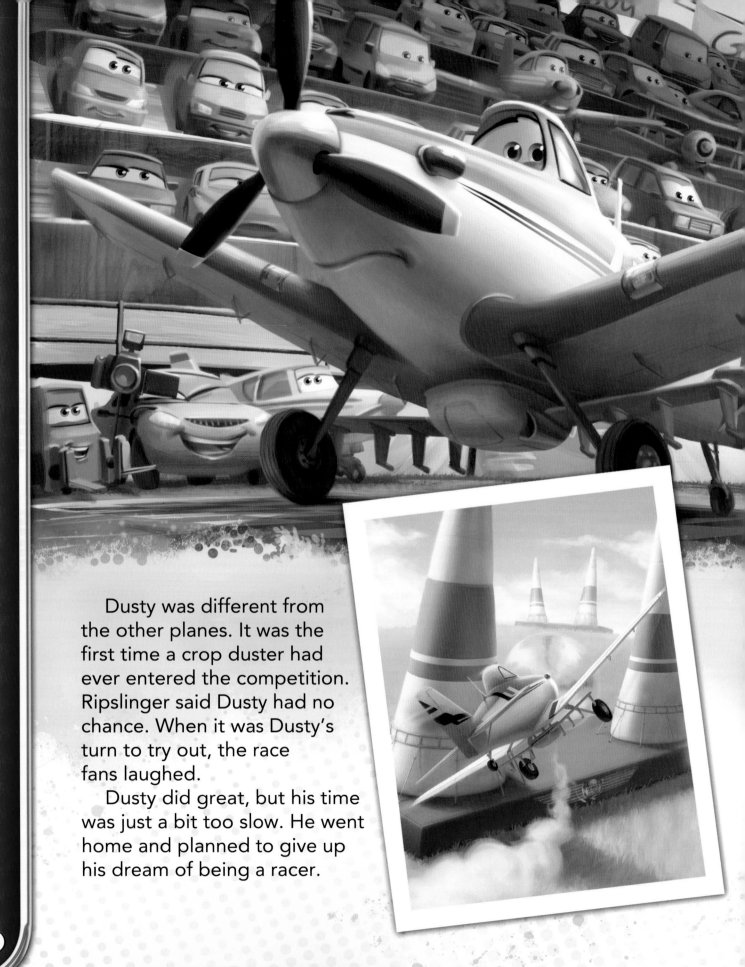

Dusty was different from the other planes. It was the first time a crop duster had ever entered the competition. Ripslinger said Dusty had no chance. When it was Dusty's turn to try out, the race fans laughed.

Dusty did great, but his time was just a bit too slow. He went home and planned to give up his dream of being a racer.

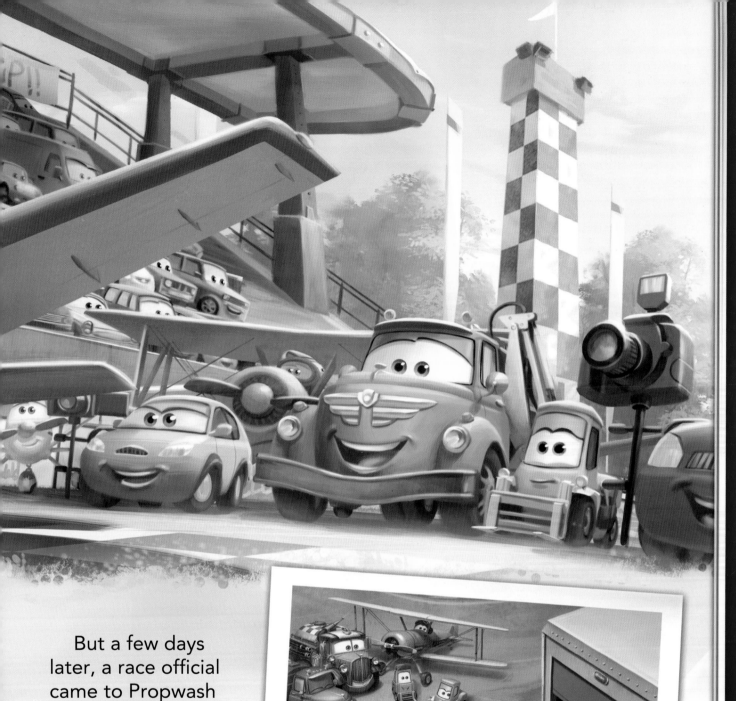

But a few days later, a race official came to Propwash Junction. He announced that the plane ahead of Dusty had dropped out. Dusty was in!

Everyone was happy for Dusty, even Skipper. He agreed to be Dusty's coach. Skipper had Dusty run shadow sprints, racing the shadows of big planes that flew overhead. "If you can beat them," said Skipper, "you just might have a chance!"

One day, Skipper told Dusty his best chance of winning was to fly high in the sky and catch the powerful tailwinds. But Dusty liked to fly low. He was afraid of heights!

The race would begin in New York City. Dusty was excited to be with the world's greatest fliers. He stopped to chat with the British racer, Bulldog, winner of the European Cup. But Bulldog was in no mood to talk. "It's every plane for himself, matey," he said.

Of course, Ripslinger was there, too. "Good luck, farm boy," he sneered.

Later, Dusty met El Chu, the indoor racing champion of Mexico. It was El Chu's first time in a long-distance rally, too.

"I will see you in the skies, amigo," he said.

The next morning, a race official gave the signal and the race was underway!

The first leg of the race was a sprint across the North Atlantic to Iceland. Right from the very beginning, Dusty struggled to keep up. A nasty hailstorm made things even worse!

But Dusty didn't give up. By the time the racers reached Germany, he was doing better. Suddenly, Dusty saw Bulldog leaking oil! "Mayday, mayday!" Bulldog called. "I can't see!"

Dusty rushed to Bulldog's side and guided him to the airport.

Bulldog was grateful. Dusty had saved his life!

Sportscasters called Dusty a hero! Suddenly, Dusty was the most popular plane in the rally. Ripslinger was angry the little crop duster was getting all the attention. He and his teammates made plans to knock Dusty out of the race.

When it came time to race across the Pacific Ocean, Skipper gave Dusty some advice over the radio. "If you lose sight of the others," he said, "just keep the sun on your right." Then, Dottie, the mechanic, told Dusty they were all going to meet him in Mexico. Dusty was excited!

Over the Pacific, Ripslinger's team broke off Dusty's antenna. Without it, Dusty was soon lost. He kept the sun on his right, like Skipper had said, but he went way off course. Dusty was almost out of gas when navy jets found him.

The jets led Dusty to the *Dwight D. Flysenhower*— the same carrier Skipper had served on. On board, Dusty learned that Skipper hadn't led hundreds of missions, like everyone thought. He'd only flown once!

With a new antenna and a full tank of gas, Dusty took off for Mexico. But he flew right into a terrible storm.

"Mayday!" he yelled into the radio. "I'm going down!"

Luckily, a rescue chopper pulled Dusty out of the water before he sank to the bottom.

Dusty, badly damaged, finally arrived in Mexico. He told Skipper what he had learned on the USS *Flysenhower*.

Skipper admitted he'd only flown one mission. He had led a squadron into a fierce battle. But Skipper was the only survivor and he never flew again. He was too afraid. Dusty turned away. Skipper had lied to him!

Dusty didn't feel like racing anymore. Besides, Dottie didn't have the parts to fix him. But the other racers had grown fond of Dusty. "Amigo, I cannot bear the thought of racing without you," said El Chu.

Ishani, the elegant racer from India, brought Dusty a spare propeller. "Perhaps it will bring you luck," she said.

One by one, Dusty's new friends gave him all the parts he needed. "This is fantastic!" said Dottie.

Dusty was back in the race!

The planes took off for New York on the final leg of the race. Ripslinger ordered his team to take care of Dusty once and for all. But just as they made their move, Skipper roared out of the sky and knocked the attackers down.

"Skipper," cried Dusty. "You're flying again!"

"Thanks to you," Skipper replied. "Now, go get 'em!"

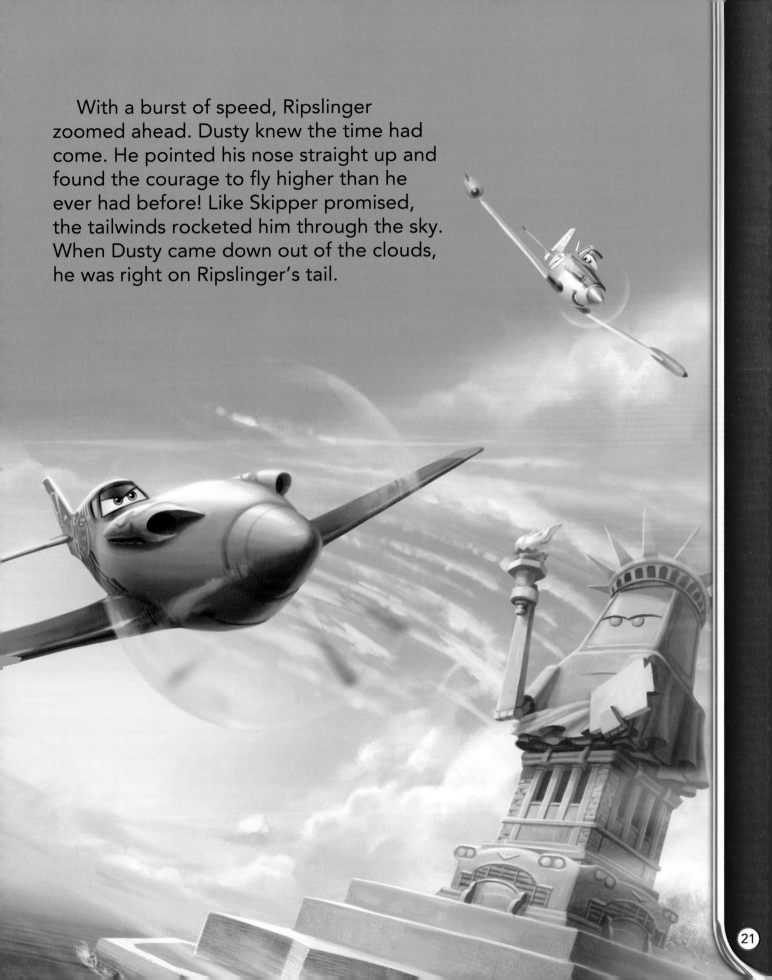

With a burst of speed, Ripslinger zoomed ahead. Dusty knew the time had come. He pointed his nose straight up and found the courage to fly higher than he ever had before! Like Skipper promised, the tailwinds rocketed him through the sky. When Dusty came down out of the clouds, he was right on Ripslinger's tail.

As Ripslinger neared the finish line, he tipped his wing. "Get my good side, fellas," he told the photographers. It was just the chance Dusty needed. He shot past Ripslinger and won the race!

Dusty Crophopper had made history. He was the first crop duster ever to win the Wings Around The Globe Rally!